Chubby Bear
and
the Noisy Night

A CHUBBY™ BEAR READER

Little Simon
Published by Simon & Schuster, Inc., New York

Plink! Plink!
Chubby Bear wakes up.
"There is a sound on my roof."

Tinkle, tinkle, tick, tick!
"That was a little noise.
Maybe a grasshopper
is hopping on my roof."

Scritchity, scriggle, pop!
"That was a little louder noise.
Maybe a frog is dancing on my roof."

Plinkety, plink, plunk!
"That was a little louder, scarier noise.
Maybe a squirrel dropped an acorn on my roof."

Crash! Vroom!
"Oh, my. That was a great, big, scary noise.
Mama Bear, an elephant is jumping on my roof.
An elephant is banging and bumping on my roof."

"My silly Chubby Bear!
That was thunder."

"And before that,
a squirrel dropped an acorn on my roof!"
"That was a branch cracking, Chubby Bear."

"And before that,
a frog was dancing on my roof!"
"Those were raindrops, Chubby Bear."

"And before that,
a grasshopper was hopping on my roof!"
"That was the wind blowing, Chubby Bear."

"I missed you, Mama Bear."
"I am here in the dark with you,
my Chubby Bear."